CLEAN Genie

Alan MacDonald

Illustrated by

Martin Remphry

OXFORD
UNIVERSITY PRESS

OXFORD
UNIVERSITY PRESS

Great Clarendon Street, Oxford OX2 6DP

Oxford University Press is a department of the University of Oxford.
It furthers the University's objective of excellence in research, scholarship,
and education by publishing worldwide in

Oxford New York

Auckland Cape Town Dar es Salaam Hong Kong Karachi
Kuala Lumpur Madrid Melbourne Mexico City Nairobi
New Delhi Shanghai Taipei Toronto

With offices in

Argentina Austria Brazil Chile Czech Republic France Greece
Guatemala Hungary Italy Japan Poland Portugal Singapore
South Korea Switzerland Thailand Turkey Ukraine Vietnam

First published in this edition 2007

British Library Cataloguing in Publication Data

Data available

ISBN 978-0-19-915188-2

1 3 5 7 9 10 8 6 4 2

Mixed Pack (1 of 6 different titles): ISBN 978-0-19-915184-4
Class Pack (6 copies of 6 titles): ISBN 978-0-19-915183-7

Printed in China by Imago

Contents

Chapter 1

The Messiest Boy in the World

Bradley Spanner was the messiest boy in the world.

His hair looked like a bird's nest. His tee shirt was always ripped. And when he ate his dinner, he dropped peas on the floor.

But worst of all was Bradley's bedroom.

Every week Bradley's Mum nagged him to tidy his room. And every week Bradley forgot.

One morning, Mrs Spanner called upstairs.

"Bradley! Have you tidied up your room?"

"Um ... nearly, Mum," said Bradley.

A minute later, Mrs Spanner put her head round the door and screamed, "Bradley! Look at this room!"

Bradley looked. His room looked just the same as ever to him. The floor was covered with toys, games and comics. There was a half-eaten apple under the bed. A dirty sock hung from the bookcase.

"What?" he asked.

"I asked you to tidy up," said his Mum.

"Oh, yeah. I forgot," said Bradley.

"You always forget. Every week it's the same."

"Well it's my room. I like it like this," argued Bradley.

Mrs Spanner ground her teeth.

"I don't like it. Tidy your room. Or I'm stopping your pocket money from today."

Bradley frowned. He didn't want to lose his pocket money.

"All right, I'll tidy up," he sighed.

Mrs Spanner pushed an old vacuum cleaner into the room.

"And when you've finished, you can vacuum the carpet," she said.

"But, Mum! I don't know how it works!" protested Bradley.

"Then it's time you learnt," said his mum.

Chapter 2
"What is Your Wish, Oh Master?"

Bradley began to tidy his room. It took him ages.

He put things into piles. One pile for his clothes, one pile for toys, one pile for books and comics. Bradley felt this was quicker than putting things into wardrobes or onto shelves.

At last, Bradley had cleared enough space to use the vacuum cleaner.

"How does this work?" he wondered. He pushed a switch. Nothing happened.

"Stupid thing!" Bradley grumbled, and gave it a kick.

At once, the vacuum cleaner whirred into life. There was a flash of light. A thick cloud of dust rose into the air.

"Woah!" yelled Bradley.

When the dust cleared, Bradley gaped in amazement.

A giant figure floated above him.

"Who ... who are you?" asked Bradley.

"I am the Cleaner Genie," boomed the genie.

"Wow!" said Bradley. "A genie! How did you get here?"

"You called me, oh Master."

The genie was wearing a white suit, and his dark hair was slicked down. His arms were folded across his chest. He looked around the bedroom and sniffed.

"Is this your room?" he asked.

"Yes," said Bradley.

"It's very messy isn't it?"

"Don't you start," said Bradley. "You sound like my mum. Anyway, I've just spent hours tidying up."

"Really? You amaze me," said the genie. He ran his finger along a bookcase.

"Dust," he sighed. "I hate dust. And it's so dusty, living in a vacuum cleaner."

Bradley wasn't interested in the genie's problems.

"Aren't you supposed to give me a wish? " he asked.

"A thousand pardons," said the genie. "What is your wish, oh Master?"

Bradley thought hard. There were so many things he could wish for. His own football team. A sweet shop.

"How many wishes do I get?" he asked.

"Just one," said the genie. "Is your room always this untidy?"

"Yes," said Bradley, crossly. "And I wish I never ever had to tidy it again."

The genie raised his hands in the air. "If that is your wish, oh Master."

"No, wait!" said Bradley. "That wasn't a wish. Though it's not a bad idea, is it?"

"I suppose not," agreed the genie.

"Just think," said Bradley, "I could be as messy as I liked. And no one would stop me."

"Be careful what you wish," warned the genie.

But Bradley wasn't listening. "I've decided," he said.

He took a deep breath.

"I wish that I never ever had to tidy my room again."

"I hear and obey, oh Master," boomed the genie.

He clapped his hands twice and spun round like a top. Thick clouds of dust rose into the air.

Bradley raised an arm to hide his eyes.

When he looked again, the genie had vanished.

Chapter 3
"A Bit of Mess Never Hurt Anyone"

Next morning, Bradley felt sure he had dreamed the whole thing.

The old vacuum cleaner stood in the corner. There was no sign of the genie.

Then his mum put her head round the door.

"I'm off to work, Bradley. Are you ready for school?"

"Yes, Mum," said Bradley, with his head in a comic.

He glanced up. The neat piles he'd made yesterday didn't look quite so neat.

"Um ... I'll tidy up later," he promised.

"Tidy up?" said Mrs Spanner. "What for?"

"You know," said Bradley. "You said I had to keep my room tidy."

His mum smiled. "Don't worry. A bit of mess never hurt anyone. Have a good day at school!"

Bradley blinked. Had he heard right? His Mum had just said she didn't mind if his room was a mess.

There was only one explanation. He hadn't dreamed it. The Cleaner Genie was real. And his wish had come true.

Bradley threw his comic in the air.

"Fantastic! I'll never have to tidy my room again!"

Chapter 4
No More Tidying

Bradley was in heaven. He had always been untidy. Now he could be as messy as he liked. And his mum never said a word about tidying up. It was wonderful.

When he took off his clothes, he dropped them on the floor.

When Bradley finished playing with a game, he left it out.

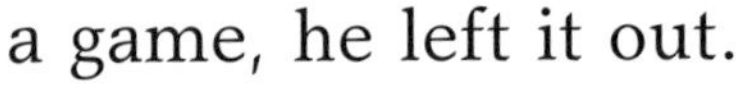

If he had got to the end of a comic, he just threw it down and reached for a new one.

His parents didn't even seem to notice. In fact, since Bradley's wish, they'd changed. They were almost as messy as he was!

His mum and dad never did any washing up. They just left the plates on the table. Soon, there were mountains of bowls and plates everywhere.

At each meal, the Spanners ate off clean plates. And when the clean plates were used up, they ate off dirty ones.

Bradley thought life was much better.

He spent more and more time in his room. He'd taken everything upstairs that he needed – TV, football, skateboard.

True, his room was getting a bit crowded. But what did that matter?

Chapter 5
Bradley's Birthday Party

A week later, Bradley raced home from school. It was a special day, his birthday, and he wanted to get ready. All his friends were coming to his house for a party.

He tried to open the front door. But it was hard to get inside. There was a pile of unopened letters on the doormat.

Next, he had to struggle past all the bikes in the hall. Why didn't anyone in his family use the shed?

Bradley found his mum in the lounge, watching TV.
"Hi, Mum!" he said, excitedly.
"Hello, love," said his mum.

Bradley stared at the room. It was a total mess. There were magazines and empty crisp packets everywhere. Piles of dirty plates filled every corner.

"Mum, aren't you going to clear up?" asked Bradley.

"Clear up? What for?" asked Mrs Spanner.

"For my party!" said Bradley. "My friends will be here soon!"

"Oh, they won't mind," said his Mum. "A bit of mess never hurt anyone."

Bradley wasn't so sure. What if one of his friends sat in a week-old pizza?

"Mum, where can my friends play? There's no space in here."

"Take them up to your room," said Mrs Spanner. "Really, Bradley! Don't be such a fuss-pot!"

Bradley ran upstairs. He'd have the party in his room. He'd have to stop his friends going in the lounge. That way, they wouldn't see the mess.

Bradley hadn't really noticed it himself, until now. But he didn't want people at school thinking he lived in a dump.

Bradley opened the door to his room.

At once, he knew he'd made a mistake.

The doorway was blocked. His stuff was piled from floor to ceiling. Bradley couldn't even see inside the room. One of his trainers fell from the top of the pile and landed at his feet.

A low rumbling sound shook the house. The huge pile of junk began to topple towards him.

"Help!" yelled Bradley.

He turned and ran. But too late. The rumbling sound behind him grew louder. A second later, Bradley was swept away in an avalanche of junk.

Chairs, books, games, toys, his bed – everything came tumbling out of his room.

Down the stairs and into the hall swept the tide of junk. It burst open the front door and finally came to a halt in the garden.

Neighbours poked their heads out their windows. They thought there must have been an earthquake.

What they saw was a mountain of junk in the Spanners' front garden. Bradley was underneath, struggling to get free.

"Oh, no!" cried Bradley. "What a mess!"

He sat on top of the pile, wondering what to do. It was half past four.

Any minute, his friends would arrive for the birthday party. How was he going to explain what had happened? How do you explain what your dirty socks and pants are doing in the front garden?

Bradley started to grab wildly at the heaps of his things.

Then his eye fell on the handle of something sticking up from the pile.

It was the old vacuum cleaner. With a great effort, he dragged it out.

Bradley took it into the hall and plugged it in.

He switched the switch. Nothing happened.

"Genie, I need you!" he shouted. Still nothing.

He gave the vacuum cleaner an angry kick.

There was a flash of light. A cloud of dust rose into the air.

Chapter 6

"You've Got to Help Me!"

The Cleaner Genie looked down at him.

"My stars!" he said. "You have made a mess!"

"You've got to help me, Genie," pleaded Bradley. "I just opened the door and it all fell out. There was too much in there."

"So I see," said the genie. "But what's the problem? You don't have to tidy it up."

"You don't understand!" cried Bradley. "My friends are coming round for my birthday!"

"Happy birthday!" said the genie, bowing.

"But it won't be happy!" wailed Bradley. "My friends will think I live in a rubbish dump! It will be all round the school."

"You should have thought of that before," said the genie, calmly.

"Can't I change my wish?" begged Bradley.

"Sorry. I did warn you. Only one wish, that's the rule."

The genie started to fade away. He was going back into the vacuum cleaner.

"Wait!" shouted Bradley. "Can't you take my wish back? Please! I'll do anything!"

The genie rose up again. He folded his arms. "Anything?" he asked, sternly. Bradley nodded.

"All right," said the genie. "I'll take back your wish. But only if you promise to keep your room tidy. And I mean tidy."

"I promise," said Bradley humbly. "This time I will, really."

"Very well," said the genie. "Stand back."

Chapter 6
Tidying Up

The genie clapped his hands twice. Then he spun round so fast that he was a blur.

Chairs, books, trousers and toys rose into the air in a whirlwind.

Bradley hung on to the front door to stop himself from being blown away. When he looked again, the house was back to normal. Everything was in its place. Everything was clean and tidy.

It wasn't a moment too soon. Seconds later, the doorbell rang. Gavin, the first of Bradley's friends had arrived for the party.

"Happy birthday, Bradley!" he said. "Are you all right? You're out of breath."

"I'm fine," said Bradley. "I've just been doing a spot of tidying up."

Bradley kept his promise. From that day on, he tidied his room every week. His mum and dad couldn't understand what had happened.

Of course, he didn't change completely. He'd promised to keep his room tidy.

But he hadn't said anything about himself ...

About the author

I once heard of a toddler who was so tidy her parents often had to rescue her clothes from the rubbish bin. Most children aren't much like that, they'd rather do anything than tidy their bedrooms.

But what would happen if you NEVER had to tidy your room? That was the question that got me thinking about this story.